Out and
About

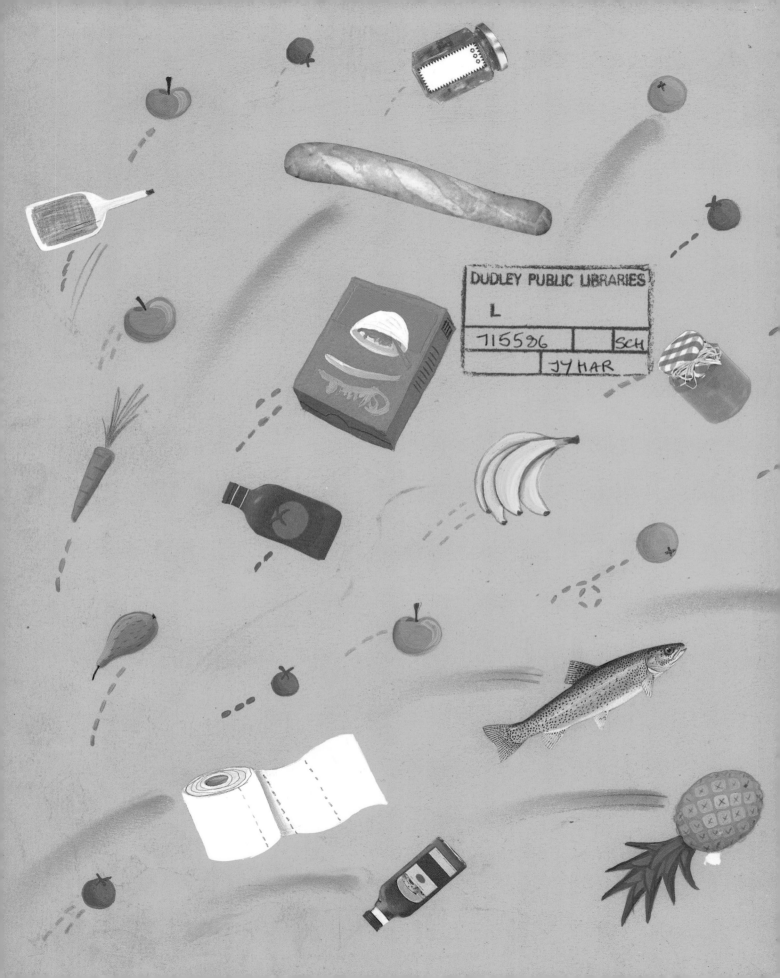

Shopping with Dad

Matt Harvey and Miriam Latimer

Barefoot Books
Celebrating Art and Story

My Mum made a list and she gave it to us,
To me and my Dad, and we went on the bus.

We got off the bus at the stop by the shop
And Dad found a trolley and —

WHOOSH!

We were off.

Dad gave me the list and the pencil to hold

And he said, 'If you're good and you do as you're told

You can cross out the things from the list as . . .

hey, wait!'

I'd already started, so he was too late. . .
'That was silly,' he said. 'Now it's quite hard to read.
This list tells me all of the things that we need.'

He read it and laughed,
and said, 'Listen to this —
Your Mum's put some very
strange things on the list:

Weatherbread, Dangerjam,

Evergreen Eggs

Octopus Underpants,

Spiders' Legs

Well-Behaved Daughter Water,

Extra-Clean Germs

Strong Anti-Grump Pills and

a Bucket of Worms

I laughed and asked,
'Does it have normal things too?'
'It does,' said my Dad.
'Now, here's what we'll do . . .'

But I didn't listen — because I was excited.
Because Mummy was funny
and I was delighted.
So I ran and I ran
and I ran and I ran.
I ran and I ran and
bumped into a man

Who was stacking up cans at the end of the aisle
Who said 'Whoa there!' and 'Steady!'
and gave me a smile.

I said, 'I'm VERY sorry.' I thought this was best
Because I knew that my Dad was getting quite stressed.
And he was. He said,
'STOP!' He said, 'Give. It. A. Rest.'

So I stopped. And I stopped. And I sat. And I stopped.
I sat there non-stop.
I stopped there and sat.
And I didn't start starting at all.
In fact . . .

I sat 'til I couldn't be still any more.
I was sitting so still it was making me sore.
It was making me feel that I couldn't quite breathe,
It was making me sweat,
it was making me sneeze.

And the sneezingy feeling it built up inside
And I just couldn't stop it —
I tried and I tried.
I tried every non-sneezingy thing I could do,
But it **Ah-!**
It just **Ah-!**
It just **Ah-Ah-Ah-**

AH-AH-CHOO

That sneeze was fantastic. It made my Dad jump
And his jump gave the woman beside him a bump,
And she went, 'Aaarrrggghhh!' and swung round in alarm
And her bag hit a woman, who jogged a man's arm

And he nudged a lady, who knocked someone else,
And the knock got passed down to the end of the shelf
Till the last person bashed the big stack the man built
Which juddered and jiggled and started to tilt . . .

And the man who'd been stacking
    turned slowly around
To see his work fall SMASH BANG CRASH
    to the ground.

SMASH BANG BONG CRASH PING
WALLOP CLUNK CLONGGG to the floor.
And everyone gasped,
and one woman swore ('Mercy!').

Then a loud angry voice said,
  'WHAT'S HAPPENING HERE?'
And I thought, 'Uh-oh,'
  and my Dad said, 'Oh dear . . .'

'It was him!' 'No it wasn't!' 'It was!' 'That's not fair!'
'She pushed me!' 'He shoved me!' 'Did not!' 'It was her!'

Then the woman my Daddy
had bumped on the arm
(The one who'd gone 'Aaarrrgggghhh'
and swung round in alarm)
She pointed her finger and said,
'It was HIM.'

And they stared at my Dad.
And my Dad scratched his chin.
And my Dad scratched his nose.
And my Dad scratched his head . . .

'But it isn't his fault that it's his fault,' I said.
'It was mine. It was me. I just, well, I sneezed.
I sort of exploded as if I was loaded
With a great big wet shout.'
Then my voice faded out . . .
They looked at me, hard, so I held on to Dad,
Who looked twenty to proud, and a quarter past sad.

And he winked at me, once,
and I looked in his face
and I saw in his eyes
the hint of a trace
of laughter,
soft laughter, that
couldn't come out,

And he said to the man who had started to shout,
'**Sssshh!**'
And he said to the people
who gave us hard looks
With a very slight shrug
of his shoulders — 'Oops!

Accidents happen,
    it's always a shame,
But when push comes to shove,
    there's no-one to blame.'

Then my Dad he got down on his knees in the store,
And he started to pick all the cans off the floor.
The woman knelt too.
        She said, 'Right. You're not wrong.'
Then everyone joined us. It didn't take long.

Dad stood up and stretched and said,
'That wasn't hard.'
So we finished our shopping.
He paid with his card.

We went home. Mum gave us a hug and a kiss.
She said, 'Did you get all of the things on the list?'
Dad told her what happened. He made it sound fun.
And she laughed and she laughed and said 'Very well done'!

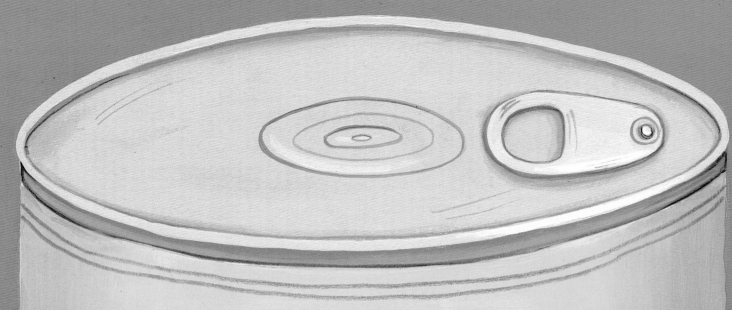

For Tom and Finn — M. H.

To my Dad, who used to bring home yummy goodies from the supermarket — M. L.

Barefoot Books
124 Walcot Street
Bath BA1 5BG

This book was typeset in 21 on 30 point Billy Serif, Handsons Hand Bold, Bob and Eddie Bounce Light,
Helvetica Rounded Bold Oblique and Jacky Bold
The illustrations were prepared in acrylics and collage

Graphic design by Judy Linard, London
Colour separation by Grafiscan, Verona
Printed and bound in China by Printplus Ltd

This book has been printed on 100% acid-free paper

ISBN 978-1-84686-171-0

British Cataloguing-in-Publication Data: a catalogue record
for this book is available from the British Library

1 3 5 7 9 8 6 4 2

Barefoot Books
Celebrating Art and Story

At Barefoot Books, we celebrate art and story that opens
the hearts and minds of children from all walks of life, inspiring
them to read deeper, search further, and explore their own creative gifts.
Taking our inspiration from many different cultures, we focus on themes that
encourage independence of spirit, enthusiasm for learning, and sharing of
the world's diversity. Interactive, playful and beautiful, our products
combine the best of the present with the best of the past to
educate our children as the caretakers of tomorrow.

Live Barefoot!
Join us at www.barefootbooks.com